Dear Pig Fans,

Pigs Will Be Pigs: Fun With Math and Money is the first title in the Pigs Will Be Pigs math series. It's all about ADDITION and PROBLEM-SOLVING! When I was in elementary school, those words frightened me, as did just about everything that had to do with math. I never realized that math was all around us in our daily lives. That's why I wrote the Pigs Will Be Pigs books, which (by the way) are all based on true family adventures. One day my family and I were in the car, ready to go out and grab a snack. When we realized we were short on cash, we decided to go back into the house and hunt for money. I had a great idea—this would be a fun way to learn about addition and problem solving using money. So follow these easy steps:

1) Read **Pigs Will Be Pigs** just for fun!

2) Go back and read the story again. Match the pictures to the words. Each time the Pigs find money, it is shown in the illustrations. Look for pennies, nickels, dimes, quarters, a fifty-cent piece, dollar bills, a two-dollar bill, a five-dollar bill, and a twenty-dollar bill.

3) Go on a money hunt at home. Identify each coin as you find it and count up how much money you've found, and then save it all in a piggy bank.

4) Answer the math questions at the end of the book. You can do this by yourself, with your parents, or with your teacher.

Remember the Pig Family Motto:

MATH + READING = FUN

DISCARD

Love,
Amy Axelrod

P.S. For Parents and Teachers
Only The Pigs Will Be Pigs books have been designed around the National Council of Teachers of Mathematics's Thirteen Standards. Use them as picture book read-alouds initially, and then as vehicles to introduce, reinforce, and review the concepts and skills particular to each title.

Pigs will be Pigs

Fun with Math and Money

story by **Amy Axelrod**

pictures by **Sharon McGinley-Nally**

Simon & Schuster Books for Young Readers

The Pigs were hungry…again.
"Let's have a snack," suggested
Mr. Pig. "Dear, what do we have to eat?"

Mrs. Pig opened the refrigerator. "Oh no! It's empty! And I just went grocery shopping this morning! Who ate up all the food?" she asked.

"B. J., Dave, and Mike helped us," said the piglets, "and Dad raided the refrigerator a few times."

"No problem," said Mr. Pig. "Let's go out to eat."

"Great idea," said Mrs. Pig, "except for one thing."

"What's that?" asked Mr. Pig.

"I didn't get to the bank and I don't have any money," she said. "Do you?"

Mr. Pig opened his wallet. "All I have is a dollar, and that's certainly not enough to feed the Pigs. Children, how about you? Any money?"

The piglets shook their heads no.

"Well, family," said Mrs. Pig, "there's only one thing to do."

"Hunt for

money!"

"Let's start with the bedrooms upstairs," said Mr. Pig.
He looked through all the closets and drawers. "Look
what I found," Mr. Pig said to Mrs. Pig. "That lucky
two-dollar bill I was saving. It was in with my socks."

Mrs. Pig searched the beds, looked under the carpet, in the night table, and in her jewelry box.

"Not too much here," she said to Mr. Pig. "Mostly a lot of dust. But I did find two nickels, five pennies, and one quarter."

Meanwhile, the piglets were busy hunting in their room. They found six shiny dimes at the bottom of their toy chest and a one-dollar bill in the bookshelf. Then they sat down to count out their penny collection….They counted two hundred pennies.

"Back downstairs, family!" said Mr. Pig.

Mrs. Pig and the piglets opened the front hall closet. They checked coat pockets and all of Mrs. Pig's pocketbooks. They found four quarters, ten dimes, one fifty-cent piece, and seventeen pennies.

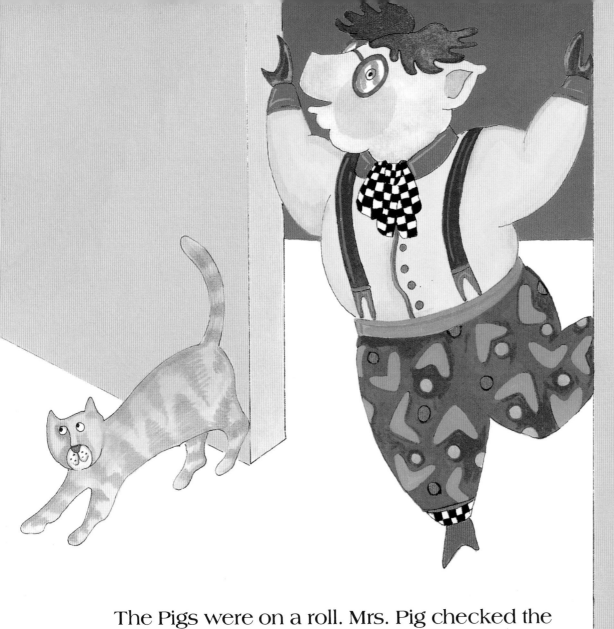

The Pigs were on a roll. Mrs. Pig checked the laundry room and found a wet five-dollar bill. Mr. Pig looked through the kitchen cupboards and pantry. "Dear," he said to his wife, "there's nothing in here. I'm going down to the basement."

A few minutes later, Mr. Pig came running up from the basement holding a twenty-dollar bill.

"Look what I found in my toolbox!" he said. "It's time to eat!"

Mrs. Pig put all of the money in a shoe box. She counted it several times while Mr. Pig drove the family to their favorite restaurant.

When they arrived at the restaurant the Pigs said to the waitress, "We're the Pigs and we're very hungry. What's the special?"

APPETIZERS

Nacho chips with salsa $ 1.50

Stuffed jalapeños $ 2.00

EGG DISHES

Huevos rancheros
ranch-style eggs
(tortillas topped with fried eggs, spicy chili sauce, grated cheese, and sliced avocado) $ 2.99

Migas
scrambled eggs with tostado
(eggs scrambled with pieces of crispy tortilla, tomato, fried pepper, onion, and garlic) $ 2.99

All egg dishes served with green-chili corn bread.

SOUPS

Black bean   Cup $ 1.25
           Bowl $ 2.25

Chef's special
(a hearty soup of potato, cheese, and green chilis)
        Cup $ 2.00
        Bowl $ 3.00

SALADS

Salad bar
Make your own tostados—top crispy tortillas with black beans, chili sauce, grated cheese, chopped tomatoes, and lettuce. Finish with sour cream.

    With dinner $ 1.99
    Salad bar only $ 2.99

Taco salad
(mixed green salad with spicy dressing in a crispy tortilla bowl)
        $ 2.99

Tax and tip included

TORTILLA SPECIALTIES

Cheese enchiladas
(3 corn tortillas filled with cheese and red chili sauce—served with southwestern rice) $ 4.99

Guacamole enchiladas
(3 corn tortillas filled with guacamole and green chili sauce—served with southwestern rice) $ 4.99

Bean burritos
(3 flour tortillas wrapped around frijoles refritos and grated cheese—served with southwestern rice) $ 4.99

Chimichangas
(3 deep-fried bean burritos topped with salsa and guacamole—served with southwestern rice) $ 4.99

MEXICAN PIZZA

Large $ 3.99
Small $ 2.99

SIDE DISHES

Colache
southwestern succotash
(string beans, corn, tomatoes,
summer squash, and hot green
chilis) $ 3.00

Calavacitas
(summer squash, corn, onions,
garlic, and chilis) $ 3.00

Quelites
(spinach and pinto beans with
scallions, garlic, and chilis) $ 3.00

Texas caviar
(marinated black-eyed peas) $ 1.50

Frijoles refritos
(refried pinto beans) $ 1.50

DESSERTS

Sopaipillas
deep-fried honey puffs $ 2.00

Flan
custard $ 1.50

Biscochitos
Mexican cookies $ 1.50

Natillas
islands of meringue on custard
                            $ 2.50

Deep-fried ice cream
(chocolate or vanilla) $ 2.00

Fresh mango/papaya $ 2.00

BEVERAGES

Cola   glass $ .75
                pitcher $ 2.00
Frozen delight
(strawberry or mango) $ 2.25

Mexican coffee $ 1.00

Regular coffee $ 1.00

Tea $ .75

TODAY'S SPECIAL

Cup of chef's special soup

Combo of:

    1 cheese enchilada
    1 guacamole enchilada
    1 chimichanga

(served with southwestern rice
and green-chili corn bread)

Unlimited visits
to our salad bar

Coconut smoothie

Sopaipillas or
deep-fried ice cream

Coffee/tea

ALL FOR ONLY $ 7.99
Tax and tip included

The Pigs ordered four specials. They ate and ate until they could eat no more. They paid the bill, then left for home.

"Boy, am I stuffed!" said Mr. Pig as he parked the car in the driveway. "I can't button my pants."

"I know what you mean," said Mrs. Pig. "I feel like I'm going to explode."

"We have bellyaches," said the piglets.

"Just a few more steps and we'll be at the front door," said Mrs. Pig. "Then we can all relax in our nice, clean, neat, cozy house. There's nothing like home, sweet home."

"Your mother's right, kids," said Mr. Pig.
"There's nothing like home, sweet…"

How much money did the Pigs find on their hunt?

Mr. Pig found

a one-dollar bill
in his wallet, $ 1.00

a two-dollar bill
in his sock drawer, $ 2.00

and a twenty-dollar bill
in his toolbox. $20.00

Mrs. Pig found

two nickels,   .05 x 2 = $ .10

five pennies, .01 x 5 = $ .05

and one quarter
in her bedroom, $ .25

and a five-dollar bill
in the laundry room. $ 5.00

Mrs. Pig and the piglets found

four quarters,   .25 x 4 = $ 1.00

ten dimes, .10 x 10 = $ 1.00

one fifty-cent piece, $ .50

and seventeen pennies .01 x 17 = $ .17
in the front-hall closet.

The piglets found

six dimes,   .10 x 6 = $ .60

one dollar bill, and $ 1.00

two hundred pennies .01 x 200 = $ 2.00
on their own.

In all, the Pigs found
thirty-four dollars and
sixty-seven cents. ————
$34.67

How much money did the Pigs spend at the Enchanted Enchilada?
How much money do the Pigs have left?

 Bonus question: Can you order other meals for the Pigs from the
Enchanted Enchilada menu? Remember they have $34.67 to spend!

For Michael, Bram, and David,
with all my love

—A.A.

. . . for friends through thick and thin—
Cupid, Elle, Diane, Ginny, Heidi, Irma, Iva,
Kathie, Lillian, Linda, Nancy, Pat, Shannon,
Virginia, and Wendy. Thank you, sisters!

—S.M.-N.

SIMON & SCHUSTER BOOKS FOR YOUNG READERS. An imprint of Simon & Schuster Children's Publishing Division, 1230 Avenue of the Americas, New York, NY 10020. Text copyright © 1994 by Amy Axelrod. Illustrations copyright © 1994 by Sharon McGinley-Nally. All rights reserved including the right of reproduction in whole or in part in any form. Simon & Schuster Books for Young Readers is a trademark of Simon & Schuster. Book design by Christy Hale. The text of this book is set in American Classic Bold. The illustrations are rendered in inks, watercolors, and acrylics. First edition. Printed in Hong Kong. 15 14 13 12 11 10 9 8   Library of Congress Cataloging-in-Publication Data Axelrod, Amy. Pigs will be pigs / story by Amy Axelrod ; pictures by Sharon McGinley-Nally. p. cm. Summary: The hungry Pig family learns about money and buying power as they turn the house upside down looking for enough money to buy dinner at the local restaurant. ISBN 0-02-765415-X 1. Pigs—Fiction. [1. Money—Fiction. 2. Finance, Personal—Fiction.] I. McGinley-Nally, Sharon, ill. II. Title. PZ7.A96115Pi 1994 [E]—dc20 93-7640